ALI BABA AND THE FORTY THIEVES

Once upon a time . . . in a distant Persian city lived two brothers called Ali Baba and Kasim. Ali Baba was terribly poor. He lived with his wife in a mud hut, and picked up sticks to sell in the market. Kasim had a rich wife and lived in a fine house.

One day, as Ali Baba was gathering sticks some way from the city, he heard a band of horsemen galloping toward him. He scrambled up a tree and hid in the foliage, seconds before a band of armed men rode underneath.

Ali Baba could tell by their evil looks that the men were dangerous, but when he saw them unloading booty from their horses, he knew they were thieves. Their leader, a grim-faced man, strode toward the base of a nearby rocky hill.

"Open Sesame!" he shouted, throwing his arms wide.

Ali Baba could hardly believe his eyes. At the thief's words, the rock face swung open to become the entrance to a dark cave. The robbers trooped inside, dragging their sacks.

Not daring to move a muscle, Ali Baba crouched in his tree. He heard the robbers' voices echoing in the cave, then out they came. Ali Baba counted them: there were forty thieves in all!

"Close Sesame!" cried the leader. The rock swung tightly shut as the robbers leapt onto their horses and galloped away.

Trembling with fear, Ali Baba climbed down the tree. Hardly aware of what he was doing, he muttered, "Open Sesame." But the rock remained still. This time Ali Baba shouted the words.

"Open Sesame!" The rock began to move.

Ali Baba lit a flare and stepped over the threshold of the cave. What a sight met his bulging eyes! Vast piles of treasure — gold and silver bowls, weapons studded with rubies and emeralds, twinkling coins, and richly-hued carpets.

He picked up a coin, his hand shaking like a leaf. "It's real!" he gasped, stunned at such untold wealth.

"I'll take some coins — nobody will every know," Ali Baba muttered, filling four bags full. When he reached home he locked the door and emptied the sacks in front of his astounded wife.

"Count them!" he ordered her triumphantly. But there were far too many coins.

"We can't count them all," said Ali Baba finally. "Run to my brother's house and ask for a corn measure."

When Kasim's wife heard this strange request, her curiosity was aroused. "I wonder what they want to measure. It can't be corn, they're far too poor." And she quickly brushed a touch of tar across the bottom of the measure. When she got it back, something was stuck to it: a gold coin!

"Now where did they get that? They're the poorest of the poor!" And she rushed off to tell her husband.

Kasim was most annoyed. "How dare my brother have gold coins without informing me?" Ali Baba innocently told Kasim his strange story, but asked him to keep it a secret.

Kasim promised, but quickly told his wife. He ordered the servants to saddle ten sturdy mules for next morning. All night long he lay awake thinking of the treasure.

It was still dark when Kasim and his mule train set out. When he reached the rock, he said the magic words and entered the cave. With beating heart, he crammed as much as he could into the saddle bags. They soon became too heavy to lift, and he realized he would have to leave some things behind. He was still picking over his treasure when . . .

. . . unluckily for Kasim, the forty thieves returned. When they saw the entrance to the cave wide open, they drew their swords and rushed into the cave. Poor Kasim was quickly discovered and slain. The ferocious robbers cut his body into quarters and left them at the entrance to the cave.

"That should warn off any other snoopers!" shouted the leader.

Kasim's wife waited in vain for two days. In desperation, she ran to Ali Baba and told him where her husband had gone.

Ali Baba, who was fond of his brother, was dismayed at the news. He saddled a mule and rode to the rock. When he saw Kasim's remains, he broke down and wept. Finally he plucked up the courage to wrap the remains in a rug, which he tied to the mule's back.

The shock was too great for Kasim's wife, who died of a broken heart. Ali Baba and his family went to live in Kasim's palace. Among the servants of the palace was Morgantina, a clever young slave girl. She told Ali Baba that his brother's remains could be put together again before being buried. Mustapha, the cobbler, would do it for a good reward.

"I'll have to blindfold you for the journey," the slave told Mustapha. The cobbler did his work well and was paid a bag of gold for his trouble. He was led, again blindfolded, back to his shop.

Meanwhile, the robber leader had returned to find Kasim's body gone. He knew that someone else had found the treasure. Angry and alarmed, he sent one of his men to the city to find out what he could. By sheer chance, the spy stopped at the cobbler's shop. Mustapha was bursting to tell someone his luck.

"... and they gave me a bag of gold for stitching the body together again."

"If you take me to the place, I'll give you another bag of gold," said the robber. The cobbler's heart sank. How was he to find the house again?

"I'll blindfold you," said the robber, "then you can take your time and try to remember which way you went."

Now Mustapha, although blindfolded the first time, had taken the precaution of counting his steps. He counted them again: "Five hundred and ten . . . eleven . . . twelve — Here!" The cobbler wrenched the blindfold off. They were standing in front of Ali Baba's palace. The robber handed Mustapha a bag of gold and, unseen, drew a red cross on the door. He hurried off to tell his leader the news.

Dusk fell, and as Morgantina was about to enter the palace, she noticed the strange mark. Her suspicions aroused, she quickly drew a red cross on all the other doors on the street.

When the forty thieves arrived they stopped in their tracks. Which was the right house?

"Fools!" cried the enraged robber chief. "Can't you do anything properly? I'll have to find out for myself!" The next day he went to Mustapha's shop disguised as a merchant. The cobbler was only too delighted to earn more gold, and took the chief to Ali Baba's door as before.

The robber chief returned to his hideout and ordered two of his men to buy a large cart and forty giant oil jars. Each of the robbers hid in a jar, except for the chief, who again disguised himself as a merchant. The last jar was filled with oil and loaded onto the cart with the others. It was late when they reached the palace. Ali Baba himself came out.

"What can I do for you?" he asked.

"I am an oil merchant," replied the chief. "It's late and I'm weary. Can you give me a bed for the night?"

Ali Baba welcomed the merchant and had the cart taken into the courtyard. He offered the robber chief a hearty meal. When it was finished, the chief excused himself, saying he must make sure none of the jars had been damaged on the journey. He went from jar to jar, whispering to his men to be ready to leap forth at his signal and kill everyone in the palace.

As the household slept, Morgantina finished her work in the kitchen. "I wonder if the merchant's oil tastes better than ours?" she said to herself, and went out to the courtyard. But when she lifted the lid from the first jar, to her horror a gruff voice growled, "Is it time yet?"

"No, not yet," muttered Morgantina hastily. At every jar, exactly the same thing happened, but the last one was filled with oil. This she dragged back to the kitchen. She poured the oil into a cauldron and heated it over the fire. Then she tiptoed from jar to jar in the courtyard, pouring boiling oil over every one of the robbers.

She hid in a corner to await events. A little later, the robber chief crept into the courtyard to give the signal. But when he raised the lids, he found to his dismay that all his men were dead. Terrified, he fled into the night.

Next morning, Morgantina told Ali Baba of her adventure.

"I'll never be able to thank you enough!" exclaimed her master. "You are an amazing girl. From this moment on, you are no longer a slave, but a free member of this household."

The robber chief, eager for revenge, shaved off his beard and disguised himself as a carpet seller. At the market he met Tabit, Ali Baba's son, who took a liking to him.

"Sooner or later this silly fellow will invite me to his father's home," said the chief to himself, "and then I can murder them all."

"That merchant sold you fine carpets very cheaply," remarked Ali Baba to his son. "Ask him to the house."

As Morgantina served refreshments, she felt sure the guest looked familiar. She realized with a shiver that the carpet seller and the robber chief were one and the same person! Morgantina carefully hid her discovery and returned to the kitchen. A little later, however, she asked if she could dance for the guest.

"If you like," said Ali Baba. When coffee was served, Morgantina entered in a swirl of veils, beating her tambourine. In her right hand she held a knife. As she stopped dancing, she plunged the knife into the carpet seller's heart.

"What have you done!" gasped Ali Baba.

"He's the robber chief!" cried Morgantina. "I know his face. He would have murdered us all!" Once again Morgantina had saved the day!

Ali Baba was the only person left who knew the secret of the treasure. He made wise use of it for many years, but he never again told anyone the magic words that would open the cave of the forty thieves.

AMIN AND THE EGGS

Once upon a time . . . a poor peasant called Amin lost all his crops in a drought. He decided to seek his fortune in another village. For the journey, he got a dozen hard-boiled eggs from a merchant, promising to pay for them later.

Seven years after this, Amin returned to his village. Now he rode a fine black horse, followed by a servant on a camel laden with gold and silver coins. Amin had become rich, and the news soon spread.

Straight away, the merchant knocked at Amin's door, asking for five hundred silver pieces in payment for the eggs. Amin refused to pay such a large sum, and the matter was taken before the judge.

The merchant appeared in court at the appointed time, but there was no sign of Amin. The judge had waited impatiently for a quarter of an hour, when Amin dashed in, out of breath.

The merchant at once put his case before the judge. "I asked Amin for five hundred silver coins, because twelve chickens might have hatched from the eggs he bought on credit seven years ago," he stated.

"These chickens would have become hens and cockerels, more eggs would have been laid, and after seven years I might have had a great flock of fowls!"

"Of course you would," said the judge. He turned to Amin with a hostile air. "What have you to say for yourself? And by the way, why are you late?"

Amin didn't turn a hair. "I had a plate of boiled beans in the house, so I planted them in the garden to make sure I'd have a good crop next year."

"Fool!" exclaimed the judge. "Since when do boiled beans grow?"

"Aha!" promptly retorted Amin. "And since when do boiled eggs hatch into chickens?"

THE TAIL OF THE BEAR

There once lived a fisherman who earned a living selling fish from door to door, making his rounds to customers on a horse-drawn cart loaded with his catch.

One cold winter day, when the fisherman was driving through the woods, a fox smelled the fish and began following the cart. The fisherman kept his trout in long wicker baskets. The fox was reluctant to jump on the cart to steal the fish, however, because the fisherman had a long whip that he cracked from time to time to spur on his horse.

At last, overcome by the enticing smell, the fox leapt onto the cart and knocked a wicker basket onto the snowy ground. The fisherman noticed nothing and continued on his way.

The happy fox opened the basket and got ready to enjoy her meal. She was about to take a first bite when a bear appeared.

15

"Where did you get that marvelous trout?" asked the bear hungrily.

"I've been fishing," the fox answered, unperturbed.

"Fishing? With the lake frozen over?" asked the bear incredulously.

The fox realized she would have to share her fish unless she could get rid of the bear. Quickly, she answered, "I fished with my tail."

"With your tail?" said the astounded bear.

"Yes, with my tail. I made a hole in the ice, dropped my tail in the water, and when I felt a bite I pulled it out and a fish was stuck on the end."

The bear touched his tail and his mouth began to water. "Thanks for the tip. I'm going fishing, too."

The ice was very thick and the bear had a hard time. Finally, his long claws made a hole. He dipped his tail into the water and waited. Evening came. The bear shivered in the cold but kept sitting with his tail in the water. Not one fish had bitten yet.

The water began to freeze. It was then that the bear felt something like a bite on the end of his frozen tail. He pulled with all his might, heard something tear, and at the same time felt a very sharp pain.

"I wonder what kind of fish is biting?" he said to himself, twisting around to look. Alas, only then did he realize that his tail, trapped in the ice, had been torn off.

And from that day to this, bears have had a little stump instead of a long, thick tail.